This book belongs to

....

LADYBIRD BOOKS
UK | USA | Canada | Ireland | Australia | India | New Zealand | South Africa

Ladybird Books is part of the Penguin Random House group of companies
whose addresses can be found at global.penguinrandomhouse.com.

www.penguin.co.uk   www.puffin.co.uk   www.ladybird.co.uk

Penguin
Random House
UK

First published 2018
002

Printed in China

A CIP catalogue record for this book is available from the British Library

ISBN: 978-0-241-32465-3

All correspondence to:
Ladybird Books
Penguin Random House Children's
80 Strand, London WC2R 0RL

FSC
www.fsc.org

MIX
Paper from
responsible sources
FSC® C018179

Peppa Loves Australia

Once upon a time, Peppa went to the airport.
She was going to visit her friend Kylie Kangaroo,
who lived in Australia.

T2

"Is it far to Kylie's house?" asked Peppa.
"Yes." Daddy Pig nodded. "It's on the other side of the world, so it takes a long time to get there – even on an aeroplane."
"Air-plane!" cheered George. George loved aeroplanes!

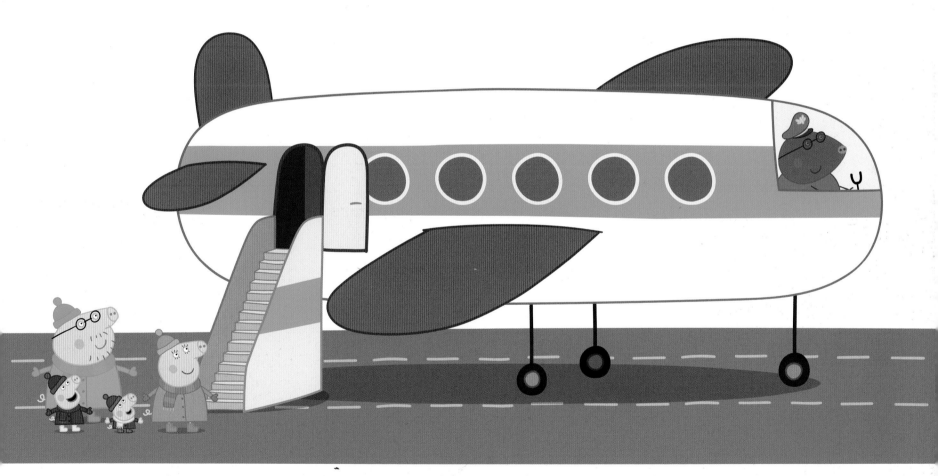

"Time to go!" called Mummy Pig.

The plane ride was exciting.
Peppa and George looked out
of the window.

They played with stickers . . .

then had some dinner . . .

and watched a film.

"What is Australia like, Mummy?" asked Peppa.
"It's an amazing country," said Mummy Pig. "It feels
a bit like home, but it is really quite different."

"I can't wait to play with Kylie," said Peppa. "I've never been to her house before."

"Daddy Pig," said Mummy Pig. "Did you remember to phone Mr and Mrs Kangaroo and tell them that we were coming?"

"Oh." Daddy Pig frowned. "I may have forgotten . . ."

After they had talked for a very long
time, Peppa and George fell asleep.

"Wake up now," said Daddy Pig. "We're here!"

"Australia is very hot!" said Peppa.
"Yes," puffed Daddy Pig. "When it's
winter at home, it's summertime here."

"Let's put on our
sun hats," said
Mummy Pig.

Peppa was very pleased to see her friend Kylie Kangaroo.

"Hello, Kylie!"
"Hello, Peppa!"

Kylie's little brother, Joey, waved to George.
"Well, this *is* a surprise," said Mr Kangaroo.

When everyone had unpacked,
Mr Kangaroo turned on his computer.

"Would you like to tell your folks that you've arrived safely?" he asked.
"Yes, please!" said Daddy Pig.

Mr Kangaroo pressed a button.
Granny and Grandpa Pig appeared.

"Granny!" Peppa gasped. "Why are you wearing your pyjamas?"
"It's night-time here," said Granny Pig.
"Australia is different to home." Grandpa Pig yawned.
"Oh yes," said Daddy Pig. "I forgot about that."

It was time to do some exploring.
Mr Kangaroo fetched his camper van.
"Climb in," he said. "There's room for everyone."
"Where are we going?" asked Mummy Pig.
Mrs Kangaroo grinned. "To the beach!"

"Yippee!" shouted Peppa. "I love the beach."

The beach was big and sandy.
Kylie jumped into the water.

Wheeeeeeee!

"Are there fish in there?" asked Peppa.
"Yes," said Mrs Kangaroo. "Our oceans
are full of incredible creatures."
Mummy Pig jumped up. "I've spotted
an incredible creature!"

"Hee! Hee!" Peppa giggled. "That's
only Daddy having a swim!"

Later on, back at Kylie's house, Peppa and George got ready for bed. They slept on an airbed in Kylie and Joey's room.

"I'm glad we came to Australia," said Peppa. "There's so much to do!"

"I expect you'll have to go home soon," said Mr Kangaroo.
"There's no rush," said Mummy Pig. "We don't fly home for weeks."

"Oh," said Mrs Kangaroo.
"I could stay here forever!"
Daddy Pig agreed.

The next day, Mr Kangaroo had a special treat
for everyone.
"Would you like to visit the bush?" he asked.

"My grandpa has a bush in his garden,"
said Peppa. "It grows blackberries."

Kylie giggled.
"Not *a* bush. *The* bush," she said.

"The bush is what we call
the countryside in Australia,"
explained Mrs Kangaroo.

The bush went on for miles. The ground was dusty and red.

"Look!"
cried Peppa. "A tree!"

"And there's
something in it!"
said Mummy Pig.

Mr and Mrs Kangaroo
got a bit closer.

"That's a koala," whispered Mrs Kangaroo.
"Koalas only live in Australia."

Peppa and George
waved. "Hello,
Mr Koala!"

It was lots of fun staying with Kylie and her family. Some days, Peppa and Kylie went out, and some days they stayed at home and played in the garden.

"Shall we play catch with my boomerang?" asked Kylie.

"Yes, please!" cheered Peppa. "What's a boomerang?"

The boomerang was a brown bendy-shaped thing. Kylie threw it into the air. The boomerang went away, and then it came back!

"Wow!" Peppa gasped.
"It's like magic!"

Peppa had a nice long holiday with Kylie.
"This is your last day in Australia," said
Mr Kangaroo. "What would you like to do?"

Peppa thought about all the things she had
enjoyed doing, like throwing the boomerang . . .

visiting the bush . . .

and meeting Mr Koala . . .

"I know!" she cried at last.
"Can we go for a picnic?"

Mrs Kangaroo nodded. "What a lovely idea."

Mr Kangaroo drove the camper van all the way back to the beach.

"I hope you're hungry!" he called.
"Do you like barbecues?" asked Mrs Kangaroo.
"Oh yes!" Daddy Pig nodded. "Let me give you a hand."

Peppa and Kylie put on their swimming costumes and sun cream.

"You go and play," said Mummy Pig. "We'll call you when the food is ready."

It didn't take long for the daddies to cook up the food on the barbecue.
"Dinner's ready!" called Mummy Pig.
"Tuck in, everyone," said Mrs Kangaroo.

"So how's that for a picnic?"
asked Mr Kangaroo.

Daddy Pig patted his tummy.
"What a great arvo,"
he replied, trying to sound
like a real Australian.

"A barbie in
our bathers!"

Ho! Ho!

Peppa and Kylie burst into giggles.
"This was the best picnic ever!" Peppa said.

Peppa loves Australia.
Everyone loves Australia!

Snort!

Hee!

Hee!

Ho!

Ho!